Born to a family tainted by vampire blood, Zora has always felt the stigma of her family's history. When history becomes vividly real as her great-great grandfather tracks her down and trades her for a blood debt owed to the local vampire king.

After her ancestor hands her over, she finds a way to trade her particular skill set for room and board in the vampire court. Her first week goes well until the king decides that she needs a warm body to relax with.

Regick has come to see the woman that his friend wishes him to heat up, and the shy miss that is surrounded by salivating shifters is what he has been looking for. Her blood will confirm if his instincts are correct, but first, he will taste the rest of her, for his own entertainment.

A dragon's blood will tell the tale, but will their one night together be enough to keep him from taking her to his lair, or will instinct win the day?

The characters and events in this book are fictitious. Any similarity to real persons, living or dead, is coincidental and not intended by the author.

Copyright © 2017 by Viola Grace
ISBN: 978-1-987969-40-5

©Cover Art/Design by Angela Waters

All rights reserved. With the exception of review, the reproduction or utilization of this work in whole or in part in any form by electronic, mechanical or other means, now known or hereafter invented, is forbidden without the express permission of the publisher.

Published by Viola Grace

Look for me online at violagrace.com, amazon, kobo, B&N and other eBook sellers.

Under His Claw
An Obscure Magic Prequel

By

Viola Grace

Chapter One

Lela felt a sense of unease as the door opened. Cool night air cascaded through the hall until it crept up her skirt.

"Lela? My love? Are you up?"

Relief flickered through her as she heard her husband's voice. "I am in the morning room, Fonso."

She looked toward the door, and the flames in the fireplace illuminated him. She could smell the alcohol on him, and his staggered steps made her sigh in resignation. Married only three months, he still sought out the local tavern more than he did her bed.

"I need you now, love."

She doubted he would be capable, but she put her sewing aside and rose to her feet. "Come to bed."

He moved with incredible speed. "No. Now."

Lela squeaked in surprise as he pinned her to the wall near the fireplace. His hand clawed at her skirt and he forced himself past her resistance, pounding against her in a fever of motion.

Lela ignored the discomfort and tried to sooth her husband by stroking his head and neck as he thrust into her. Instead of the heat, which normally filled his body with each rock of his hips, he was getting colder.

The scent of blood filled the air, and it was not from his rough treatment of her; she saw the slow flow pumping out of the two puncture marks in his neck.

He looked at her, and she saw the red

Under His Claw

---

flames flickering in his eyes. "One last time, Lela."

He shuddered and arched against her, throwing his head back and showing his newly lengthened teeth.

Tears in her eyes streaked down her cheeks as she drew back her hand and snapped his head back. He dropped like a stone and she scrambled free of him, his seed trailing down her thighs under her skirt, cold and icy.

Lela flipped her sewing chair and pulled out the two silver blades her mother had gifted her with on her wedding day. In no nightmare had Lela ever imagined using them against her husband.

"Lela, Lela, my dear gypsy bride. You don't think I married you to have your blood mix with mine in my children, now did you? You were always destined for sacrifice."

She held the blades down at her sides

in the folds of her skirts and watched him straighten his head and stand up with an unnatural motion.

"Why then?"

He turned toward her, his golden hair ruffled and his amber eyes glowing with red fire where his soul should have been. "Ah, gypsy blood is strong. The best thing for one of my kind to start their new life on is gypsy blood."

"I am your wife."

"And yet another reason you have to die, Lela. The wedding was only to keep you with me while I waited for my master to consummate the change. I cannot be a rising vampire with a living relative. Not in today's age of vampire politics where everyone watches for weakness. I am afraid your bloodless body will be thrown from the parapet. Your awkward life as a filthy gypsy amongst good people will have become too much for you, and no one will mourn." He stepped to-

Under His Claw

ward her in a rush.

When he caught her in his arms, two blades stopped him. He staggered back, and she cut his face, slicing her fear and devastation into his flesh.

She kept cutting, working at him until he was on the floor in a quivering heap. "You never could stand to go up against a prepared opponent. You will leave me alone, and I will sign an annulment. We have no children and the local priest is carrying the documents with him. It will be done before I leave town, but do not think you can ever take my blood."

The handsome man that had swept her off her feet lay there hissing and twisting as his skin reformed with red welts where the silver had burned him. She pressed the heel of her boot into his palm and stripped off the wedding band that her family had offered him.

"Tell me now that you will never seek out me and mine and I will give you what you need."

He blinked in confusion. "What do you mean?"

"To gain your position, to fix your change, you need to consume gypsy blood. I will give you what you need and leave it in a goblet next to the fire. What you tell your sire is up to you."

"You would do that for me?"

"I would do it to cut ties between us. Swear it. You will never come after me or mine."

"I will never come after you or yours."

She nodded and sliced him a few more times, running to their chamber to gather what she could. Jewels, clothing and a set of pistols were tucked away before she returned to the morning room where he was staggering to his feet.

Lela set a goblet down and sliced her left palm, bleeding into the cup until it was full. She bound her wound and faced Alfonso's hungry expression.

Under His Claw

"Take it and never speak my name again."

He dove for the cup. She escaped the house through the underground tunnels; the sire would have put watchers on their house.

The sudden flare and flicker of light behind her told her what she needed to know. Her home was gone, and he was hiding the fact that she was not.

The flames made her smile through the tears of disappointment. She had imagined a life with him, a family, and he had only wanted her as a sacrifice. Lela looked around at the empty marshlands and closed her eyes, finding her family. They would not take her in as a member now that she had broken with them, but they would protect her and let her live on the outskirts of their caravan.

She would start her life anew as a pariah, but she would be alive.

* * * *

One hundred and twenty-four years later

Zora shivered in the rain and looked up and down the open street before she crossed. She always tried to get home before sunset, even though the dark siders were supposed to abide by the standard daylight laws. There was always a look in their eyes that said they might not feel like playing by the rules for a night.

She walked down the street with her head bowed as she tried to avoid getting soaked, even though she was fairly sure she couldn't get any wetter.

She sidestepped an oncoming woman with brilliant green eyes and didn't look over her shoulder to continue trying to figure out what she was. The feel of the gaze on her spine let her know it was some sort of predator.

Getting to her building didn't make things any easier. A hunched shadow sat near the door, and she opened the outer door with a practiced twist, turning to pull it closed behind her.

Zora climbed the three floors and wished for enough money to be able to afford a building with an elevator. She opened her door and closed it, latching all nine locks, one at a time.

There was no dignity to squelching across her tile floor and stripping in the bathroom, but the hot shower felt amazing.

An hour later, she was sitting in a long-sleeved jersey dress with a glass of wine and the wreckage of her dinner next to her. She flipped through the channels and was just settling in for a Friday of investigative television when a knock sounded at her door.

Zora looked over at the door with irritation. "Who is it?"

The knock sounded again.

Zora pulled a shawl around her shoulders to hide the fact that underwear had not been on the evening's agenda, crossed the room and looked through the peephole. A pair of red eyes stared back at her.

"Tsura Charani Maloney?"

Zora stepped back, away from the door. No one called her Tsura. No one was supposed to know the name. She was Zora Charity Maloney on all of her legal documentation.

The door rattled in the frame, and Zora ran to get her great-great grandmother's blades. Cutting a vampire went against everything she had inherited, but it was her only chance.

She held up the knives her great-great grandmother had used to fend off her husband, and she backed up against the wall. Her confidence that a vampire couldn't come into her home without her permission was shattered when the door burst in.

He was tall, lean and elegant, but it was her resemblance to the face she saw in the mirror that filled her with horror. The scars on his face sealed the resemblance to her ancestor. "That's impossible."

"Why? I am your blood, darling, and you are mine. It is about to make me a very happy man." He rushed her, and before she could get her knives up, he had clamped a hand over her mouth and nose, making soothing sounds as her lungs screamed and her world went black.

Chapter Two

She was being carried, and her senses were vibrating with the nearness of a gathering of vampires. For over two decades, Zora had fought what her senses were telling her, but now, there was no choice. She was in danger and her life was about to take a sudden shift.

Zora opened her eyes just enough to see and looked at the elegantly dressed men and women around her. She tried to keep her breathing calm, but her heart was pounding in a staccato beat.

"Easy, child. This will be over shortly. We have to wait our turn."

She whispered as softly as she could.

Under His Claw

"How did you find out about me?"

He chuckled. "The Internet is an amazing thing. Genealogy websites are just fascinating."

She winced at the thought that one of her distant cousins had plugged her name into a display for everyone to see she was related to this monster.

He stepped forward, and she took in the line he appeared to be in. A deep, booming voice was speaking and a lighter voice was pleading. There was a whistling sound and a *thwack*, and then all was silent until the deep voice spoke again.

They were moving up a very disturbing line.

The woman in front of them asked for, and was granted, a larger territory to look for humans who wished to act as food. She went away quite happy.

The room went completely silent when her great-great grandfather stepped forward.

"Alfonso, you have come to pay what is due to me?" The deep voice was raspy, but it carried throughout the room.

"Your majesty, I have brought you what is due to you. My blood."

Zora was set on her feet, and she straightened her shawl before looking at the man in front of her crafted of ivory and obsidian with ruby eyes.

"I will rip you apart for lying, Alfonso." The words fell as casually as if he was discussion fashion.

Alfonso shoved her forward. "Taste her, your majesty. She is of my blood. My spawn."

Zora stumbled and caught herself inches from the creature radiating power.

A long and elegant hand reached out, lifting her chin to force her to face the ruby red gaze. She flinched when the weight of the vampire's mind pressed against hers. She fought back memories of being chased by the blood drinkers who nearly killed her mother, but he lifted them one by one and examined them. Her secret was laid bare to him, and he laughed.

The fingers held her up under her chin, and her captor looked to her ancestor. "She is an acceptable alternative, but you will leave my territory tonight and never return."

Alfonso sounded frantic, "Your majesty!"

She was released, and she fought the urge to step back as the vampire king rose to his feet. His voice was a dark whisper. "Go, now, before I keep her and take the blood I was promised."

Zora heard scuttling behind her, and at a nod, a woman came to her side and led her out of the audience chamber. Zora didn't know where she was going, but she had no interest in remaining in the room. Anything different was preferable.

The room she was settled in was far quieter and only had two other vampires in it. The woman smiled gently. "His majesty will be with you in a moment. He is finishing up the petitions."

"Which vampire king is it? I am not even sure what city I am in."

"His majesty's name is Olvadi, though you are not to speak it. Address him as 'your majesty' or 'your lordship'. You are in the shadow city of Arbor."

She sighed. She was only two cities away from home. "When can I leave?"

The woman blinked. Her red and blue eyes were surprised. "You are not leaving. You have been traded to his lordship to save your ancestor's life. You belong to the crown now, in whatever capacity he chooses to employ you."

Zora shook her head. "It is impossible. I am a free human with my own life

Under His Claw

and a job and everything. I can't be stuck here."

She stood up, and the woman placed her hand on her shoulder and forced her back onto the settee.

"By the laws of the dayside government and the nightsiders, you can be used to pay for the debts of your family members. There is a little-known amendment that makes it so."

Zora gritted her teeth. "I want to see it."

A blur of motion heralded the king's arrival.

"And so you shall. If your abilities are real and not the fevered imaginings of a young woman, you shall be given a place at my side and a revered post in my cabinet."

Zora flinched as he removed his shirt, exposing burned-in crosses and scars left by consecrated silver. "What if it doesn't work?"

He shrugged and sat on an ottoman near her. "Then, I will take the blood promised by Alfonso. He is right; you are of his line."

She flexed her hands nervously. "What now?"

He gave her a smile that showed a lot of teeth. "Now, you heal at least one of these marks, and if you are successful, I let you live. If not, Octavia is standing by."

Zora looked at the ivory skin and the deep pitting of a holy-water wound. "I will need a knife and a towel, and some gauze and bandages for afterward."

He chuckled. "For you or me?"

"The towel is for you." She tried to stop her hands from shaking. "I will need everything else."

He nodded slightly, and one of the men disappeared, reappearing in a minute with all the items.

Zora was a little disturbed at how easily accessible the first-aid kit was, but she put it aside and laid everything else out next to her. "Did you see how this works?"

"I did. It seems fascinatingly implausible."

She licked her lips and looked him in the eyes. "Did you see what happens if you drink from me?"

"If you can do what you promise, it will not be an issue. No one will drink from you under my protection." His words hung in the air, and his inner circle seemed to absorb them.

"Do you want privacy for this? It will be painful. The same pain which caused the wound will be woken when I heal it."

He looked around. "This is privacy. I am never without at least three guards."

Zora lifted the knife and opened it, feeling everyone in the room tense. The blade clicked into position easily, and it appeared wickedly sharp. She lifted her hand and pressed the blade to her skin until it parted. When blood flowed, she lifted the knife and scored her skin again. When her palm was filled, she looked toward her patient and pressed the blood to the ancient wound.

His muscles stiffened and he gritted his teeth as her blood bonded to his skin, crept under it and forced the damage up and out.

Zora kept her hand on him, and she whispered, "The towel please, in my right hand."

She dropped the knife, and Octavia handed her the towel, a horrified expression on her face.

Zora blotted up the blood and the water, which came out of his skin; she held on until she felt the whole flesh beneath her hand. With a gasp, she pulled away and wiped his chest, exposing the new, whole skin where the jagged pit had been.

Under His Claw

Her hands shook as she worked to clean the cuts. She healed quickly, but having an open wound was never a good idea. The first-aid kit contained a series of wipes, and she used them to clean up.

Her patient was stroking his chest, marvelling at the segment that was now unblemished. Vampires were vain, and the marks left by torture early in their nightlives were irritating in the extreme. Her peculiar ability to heal vampires had manifested when she was five, and it had disrupted her life from then on out.

Zora was wrapping her hand with gauze, fastening the pad down, when two large pale hands took over, and the vampire king finished wrapping her wound. He made it snug but not tight, and she blinked in surprise at the scent coming off his hair. He smelled like open prairie, which was not a smell she associated with vampires.

When he taped it in place, he patted it

lightly before turning the burning ruby gaze on her once again. "How long until you can do it again?"

"Once a day is best. Every two days is better. Smaller wounds can be healed at the same time, but only a wound the size of my hand can be healed at once if it is a deep wound."

He cocked his head. "You claim to have healed dozens, but I have never heard of you before."

She swallowed. "There is a reason for that. The clutch of nightsiders which kept me prisoner and had me heal them; my mother killed them all and burned their nest to the ground."

He reached out and stroked her hair with his icy hand. "I can understand why. Such a treasure."

She stared into his eyes, and she knew without doubt that he wasn't going to let her out of his sight. Zora was now the healer to the vampire king of Arbor.

Under His Claw

She wondered what the dental plan was like.

Four days later, she was standing beside the throne in a designer suit and heels with the bangles of ownership on her wrists. Her apartment had been cleared out, and all of her information had been registered with the nightsider government. She was officially in the employ of the vampire king, and when it came to vampires, *employee* meant possession.

Three days had healed some of the more obvious marks on Olvadi. It had also been enough time to witness a portion of the full debauchery of the dark court.

Her days took on a pattern. She woke around two, got showered and dressed. Ate and, to her surprise, she was responsible for some of the communications of the vampire king. She was now one of an army of flunkies who had to make calls on behalf of Olvadi, invitations accepted and declined.

Speaking to other nightsiders at gatherings was odd. Like anyone else, she had seen shifters on the news and felt certain she had seen them on the street, but actually calling their prides, clans, covens and coalitions was bizarre.

By the time the vampires rose, all the calls were made, the living ate again, brushed their teeth and attended the evening events in whatever capacity they were hired for. Zora wanted to make friends with some of the girls with a pulse, but they were hired as decorative food, and it felt like talking with a ham with good fashion sense.

Octavia was usually at her side, with Wilhelm and Michael nearby. Octavia had been granted a reconstruction on the second day. Zora hoped to work on her other breast at a later time. Two

Under His Claw

hundred years ago, many rural areas had not been so accepting of vampires and Octavia had met an inquisitor who didn't like women. It was hard to see her new companion's joy over regaining what should never have been taken.

After petitions, everyone changed and the true dark court took over. No government members, no outside humans, just the vampires and shifters enjoying an evening. Thankfully, the king only dragged her to it on her second night. Casual nudity was not something Zora was familiar with before that night, but she was definitely familiar with it after.

That night, she was standing behind Olvadi and trying not to watch the shifters in the crowd. A few of the bolder men had sniffed her and pronounced her *tasty*. It wasn't a description she was comfortable with.

Zora fidgeted a little, and Octavia gave her a stern look. Zora sighed and remained still with her hands folded in front of her.

The petitioner was asking for permission to marry, and the young man at his side looked pleased and nervous.

Olvadi leaned forward. "Come here, child."

The young man quivered with eagerness, but he obeyed, kneeling in front of the vampire king.

Zora tried not to roll her eyes.

"Do you have children, Antony?"

The young man whispered, "No."

"Are you of age?"

The young man's eyes flickered, and even Zora could see the lie before it came out. "Yes."

Olvadi leaned back with a sigh. "Petition denied until he is twenty years of age, Leonard. You know the rules. It may have been acceptable at the turn of the century, but now, you must wait for eighteen months before you can reapply."

"But, your majesty, he is willing." The older vampire whined.

Olvadi looked at the petitioner. "And we have a treatise. Eighteen months and if you turn him before then or take him to another kingdom, you both end as ashes. Am I clear?"

Antony pleaded, "But he won't love me if I am older."

Olvadi smiled, leaned forward and stroked the young man's hair. "Then, it is not love but lust, and you can both find better partners for it."

It was the last petition of the night, and Zora sighed with relief. If she were lucky, it would be another healing night.

The court was dismissed, the king and his attendants filed out. When Octavia took Zora to her room and pulled out a wrapped chiffon gown, Zora winced. "Please tell me I don't have to watch the orgy again."

"Olvadi wants you to take a lover. Since we cannot have you with a vampire, we need to select one of the shifters for you."

Zora froze as Octavia undressed her. "You said what now?"

"A lover. You overreact and have no emotional outlet amongst our kind, so Olvadi wishes you to have one from the upper rankings of the shifters. He would offer you to the elves, but they are disturbing in the extreme. I am not sure you are up to the stresses of having an ancient being as a lover."

"Stop saying lover." She shivered in her new silk underwear and lifted her arms for Octavia to drop the dress over her head. Being dressed was something she had gotten used to over the last few days. Octavia could move more quickly than she could, and when the zipper went up, she stepped back and circled Zora so quickly the skirts flared.

"Take a look."

Zora looked in the mirror, and as she watched, Octavia braided her hair into a loose coronet and pulled tendrils out to cover her neck with light wisps of dark hair. It was more of a tease to the vampires than it was an actual covering. The gown was black at the hem rising to a green around her waist, which brightened to emerald at her shoulders. It made the amber of her eyes brighten in intensity, and her black hair gave her skin an ivory cast. She could pass for a vampire if no one watched her move.

Octavia disappeared and reappeared in a cut-out evening gown a minute later.

"Why a lover?"

"Because you flinch at our touch. Now, shall we go?"

It wasn't really a question, so Zora went.

Chapter Three

Subtle music filled the air and dancers cavorted on wide tables. If not for the clothing, it could have been a scene out of ancient Rome.

Zora and Octavia followed Olvadi and the other two bodyguards to the head table. Zora sat on his right, Octavia on his left.

A tiny crystal glass full of blood donated by one of the employed humans was placed in front of Olvadi. He lifted it to his lips and inhaled briefly before drinking. Everyone relaxed, and the music picked up in cadence and volume while food was provided for the vam-

Under His Claw

pires and the others in attendance.

Olvadi took Zora's hand in his, and he spoke, "So, Zora. Which one would you like to have sex with?"

She blinked rapidly. "What?"

Even forewarned, she thought she had more time to think of a way to dissuade him.

"Warm bodies need contact to remain emotionally healthy, and since contact with vampires disturbs you, you will take one of the shifters here as your lover. They have all agreed to honour your choice."

She blinked. "They have agreed?"

Olvadi waved his hand around the room.

Zora noted a lot of faces turned toward hers. "They have all been invited here because of their position and attractiveness. Octavia selected them all."

"I don't want to."

His hand tightened into an icy cuff.

"You will choose, or they will. If they have to fight for your attentions, I cannot guarantee your safety, and since I have guaranteed your safety, I am ordering you to choose one of these men and take him to your room tonight. I will know if you have not followed my orders. You will not like the result."

She swallowed at the fire in his eyes. He had been almost fatherly toward her over the last few days, but apparently, it was over.

"Now?"

"Now. Octavia will help you make your choice. She will conduct the introductions."

Zora swallowed and got to her feet.

Octavia mirrored her and came to her side. "Do not worry. It is a simple thing. In the morning, he will have gotten his way and you won't have to worry."

"Oh goody. Simply one night of humiliation."

"No one you don't want. Let me help you pick, and you will not be disappointed."

Octavia had seemed to have a slight big-sister streak when it came to Zora, or so it had appeared. It was going to be a trust issue, but at least she was confident none of the shifters would do permanent damage.

Octavia bypassed a few who had a predatory gleam in their eyes and introduced her to a wolf, a tiger and an eagle.

Albertus, the wolf, took her hand and pressed a kiss to the back of it. "It is a delight to meet you. If I am chosen, I promise you a fascinating evening."

She swallowed and smiled weakly. "A charming offer. I will consider it."

Raynard, the eagle, gave her a sneering glance, which had her stomach flipping with unease. He kissed her hand as well and looked her over. "Not as thin as I had hoped, but you will do."

Zora jerked her hand back. "You won't. Thank you for coming."

He gripped her arm and pulled her toward him. "You misunderstand. I was invited to fuck you."

Octavia struck him in the chest, and it sent him flying back into a crowd watching an orgy.

Conrad, the tiger, supported her by the elbow. "Are you all right?"

She blinked and smiled weakly. "Yes, thank you."

There was a disturbance in the entryway, and Zora looked to the king. He lifted his hand, and the tawny-headed contingent strode in and came over to greet him.

It seemed a fairly even meeting, but the two males were sizing each other up. They spoke softly, and Olvadi nodded in her direction. When the other man turned to look, she looked at Conrad and smiled brightly. "So, did you come here

Under His Claw

strictly to meet me? I am flattered."

Conrad was handsome, dark haired and he had the loveliest blue eyes she could have ever imagined. Her body warmed at the thought of him on her and inside her. For one night, he would be more than enough.

She opened her mouth to ask him to come with her when a hand tapped her on the shoulder. She was whirled around, and a mouth closed on hers. Heat bloomed the moment she tasted him. Her heart pounded, and she felt herself being bent backward.

The smell of warm male swirled around her, and she held onto his arms for balance as her senses were spinning for purchase.

When he held her upright and released her, he was grinning and her heart was pounding. "Pardon my tardiness. I am Regick, invited shifter."

Octavia was in the background making a negative motion.

Zora turned to Conrad, but he was gone, as were the other offered suitors. She frowned at Regick, "What did you do to the others?"

He smiled. "Nothing, nor did they want me to. I have heard you are in the market for a companion for the evening."

She blinked and looked around again with an air of desperation. Olvadi caught her gaze, and he nodded his head toward Regick.

Softly she whispered, "I suppose I am."

"Would you care to go for a walk in the lower gallery? The portraits there are stunning."

She looked around again. "I was supposed to—"

"In good time. We have all night, and Olvadi isn't getting any older. He will wait until he rises tomorrow before you

Under His Claw

will be put to the question."

Zora was still wrapped in his arms, and she had no choice when he began walking through the crowd, and it parted for them. Whatever he was, even the vamps moved around him.

He led her down the grand staircase and into the gallery. While she hesitated, he had no such restraint. He simply kept his arm behind her and walked with her to the gallery, two vampires trailing behind them.

"You seem to have landed in a peculiar position, miss."

Regick chuckled and paused in front of an image of Olvadi destroying a village in his younger days as a crusader.

"Zora. Call me Zora."

"Zora, then. You haven't been here long."

She shook her head. "Less than a week."

"Why is Olvadi taking care of you by

finding you a companion?"

She blushed. "Why don't you ask him?"

"Oddly enough, he can be very stubborn for a creature who has passed ten centuries. He is taking excessive care with you, though. It is interesting."

She shrugged. "I am useful, I suppose. I was sold to him for the life of one of my ancestors."

Regick winced. "Ouch. A blood feud that goes back that far?"

"No. My great-great grandfather was a dick. He kidnapped me and exchanged me for his freedom. Blood for blood."

The vampire nearest her cleared his throat.

She sighed. "And that is the end of conversation about me. You were invited here?"

"A favour in exchange for a favour. It was more of a command performance."

She cocked her head. "You don't seem

the type to give in to commands easily."

He chuckled. "You know me well already?"

"No, but there is something about the way you clear the space around you, which tells me you are used to doing what you like. I had a teacher like you once. He wasn't cruel, but he did lay things out in a no-nonsense way."

Regick chuckled. "I have never been compared with a teacher before. I don't know whether to be flattered or check my wardrobe."

She glanced at the pristine shirt and immaculate slacks he was wearing. "Well, if upstairs is any standard of measure, you are overdressed for an orgy."

He chuckled. "I do not participate in the vampire festivities. I find the touch of the cool flesh disturbing."

She swallowed and he caught on.

"So that is it. You can't stand their

touch."

She shivered and stepped back, crossing her arms and rubbing her biceps to shake off the shiver. "I can't imagine it intimately, if it makes sense."

"It makes sense." He put his arm around her, and they continued their slow walk down the gallery of vampires in historical moments. Crossing the ocean-wearing cloaks and huge-brimmed hats, stepping foot in North America for the first time. The initial treatise with the natives that set the vampire foothold in the new world. When the human colonists arrived, the nightsiders already had a strong presence, and they crafted the rules and regulations. Their society had evolved into predators and prey living side by side in the cities, and the towns surrounding them were usually one or the other.

The rest of the images were vampire kings and queens breaking ground at

Under His Claw

their palaces, portraits of courts and the memorable moments of modern day.

She was becoming used to the scent and feel of Regick, and Zora clued in that this walk was actually foreplay. His fingers cruised over her back and ribs so lightly she didn't even notice she was leaning into his touch.

Zora laughed lightly. "You are very good."

He grinned down at her, and his amber eyes glowed in the dim light. His hard jaw and the sensual curve of his lips kept her attention as he lowered his head to hers. "Who told?"

She giggled, and he pressed his lips against hers, stroking her tongue with his. The rough texture and heady taste of him had her head spinning again.

He lifted his head and whispered against her lips. "I won't hurt you, I will take care to ensure your pleasure and your safe word will halt all interactions between us."

Zora closed her eyes and then opened them, meeting his gaze. "Carter is my safe word."

He smiled and nodded. "An easy one not to mistake."

"And easy to pronounce while distracted."

"Well, then, as the rules have been spoken, shall we?"

Zora nodded nervously, her muscles tense and her mouth dry. "My rooms are up two levels and down the hall."

"Then, we had better make our way."

Again, he kept an arm around her and proceeded up the steps with her guards trailing after them. She was an asset, and she needed to get used to being treated as such.

When she had directed him to her room, he eased her inside and then closed and threw the bolt on the door.

He shrugged. "It won't actually hold

Under His Claw

them off, but it will annoy them."

Zora retreated to lean against her desk, and she held onto her chair with both hands behind her back. She licked her lips nervously.

Regick's focus was on her mouth. He matter-of-factly removed his cufflinks and worked on his shirt until it hung open, exposing bare chest, which was crisscrossed with scars.

The body hair on his chest had her fingers curling more tightly around the chair back. Out of vanity, the vampires shaved completely from neck to toe. There was not a chest hair to be found in the king's court.

Regick was a contrast to everything around him, and Zora's curiosity got the better of her. She released the desk and stepped toward him, flattening her hands on his chest and stroking the hair she found there.

His hands came around her shoulders, and he stroked her back. The cool air of the zipper opening caused a flutter of arousal in her pussy. It was strange what she wanted. She used to want to be alone, but now, with her body constantly surrounded, she wanted to be alone with one other person, and here he was.

Regick eased her dress off her shoulders, and it caught on her hips. Her silken slip was all that separated her skin from his. He ran his fingers over her exposed back and the silk. "You are softer than the silk."

"You don't need to flatter me. I am a sure thing."

He didn't like it much. Her skirt hit the floor and he tossed her to the bed. "Well, since I don't need to exude effort..."

She skidded along her sheets with her silk chemise easing the friction of her slide.

With short, angry movements, Regick

Under His Claw

removed his shirt, shoes, socks and trousers. He might be irritated, but his erection was long and hard, arching insistently upward. He grabbed her thighs and pulled her to the edge of the bed, forming claws and tearing her chemise from her. The small scrap of panties she wore was torn off with equal irritation.

Naked and staring up at an insistent male, she held her hand up and said, "No."

"No, what? You said you were a sure thing. Obviously, you only want me to fuck you and leave."

Tears began to flow. "No. It wasn't what I meant. I don't want this, but I don't want pain or a joining without attachment. I am scared."

He sighed and pulled her upright, sitting on her bed and pulling her across his lap. "Why are you scared?"

"I don't do this a lot."

He chuckled. "A woman's body is a

remarkable design; you were meant to take a lover."

She wiped her tears and controlled her breathing. "Everything about this place scares me."

It seemed that having a man in her room had been enough to break her hard-won calm. She swallowed hard.

"Good, it is a frightening place. It shows you are sane."

"But for how long? I have tonight with someone I can touch, who will touch me back with hands which are warm and skin that doesn't feel like cold porcelain."

She looked up at him and was sure she looked horrible. She knew her eyes were red and her skin was blotchy, but he stroked her cheek and tugged at the tendrils of hair on her neck. Zora felt the caress of claws on her neck, and she swallowed nervously.

"Do you trust me?" He stroked his

hand down her skin, the delicate scrape of his claws giving her flickers of pleasure through the threat of pain.

"I don't know you."

He smiled, and she could see deadly fangs growing in his jaws. He carefully enunciated, "Do you trust me?"

She looked into his amber eyes and nodded. "I think I... yes. As much as I trust anyone."

"Then, allow me to show you what those cuffs are designed for."

He rose to his feet with her in his arms and centred her on her bed. He used his clawed hands to grasp her wrists, and he pressed them up to the headboard.

Zora heard small clicks, and she tugged at her wrists. The bands were locked inches above her head, holding her arms up and out of the way. "What..."

Regick looked down at her with a

sharp smile. "Sex with a shifter is a dance of dominance and submission. You are not trained to hold me down, so I will ease my instincts by making you helpless."

She twisted her wrists, and the metal snapped tight, holding her fast.

He chuckled. "And now there will be no struggles."

She sighed and swallowed. "I still want you."

She saw his eyes flare from human to slit-pupil and back again. His teeth made the kiss awkward, but no less arousing as he covered her body completely, and he rubbed his skin across her in a full-body caress.

There was no going back.

Chapter Four

Regick was careful with his claws, but they were a deadly reminder he wasn't a normal human male. They folded back when he wasn't using them and extended when he flexed his hand.

Zora was grateful that he didn't tell her to relax. Either it would happen or it wouldn't.

Locked in place, she was able to appreciate the width of his shoulders and the deliberate care he was taking with her. The light scratching was waking the surface of her skin, and she could feel herself getting wet as he stroked over spots on her skin that were exceptionally sensitive.

When he drew his fingers under her navel, she gasped and her muscles tightened. He continued his stroking and made it down to her thighs. Her inner thighs slid together, but he inserted a leg between them. She was open to him. He stared into her eyes while he drew his deadly fingers up. She shivered as his light stroke slowed as it closed in on her sex.

He stroked two fingers through the slick heat she was giving him, and she closed her eyes as he lifted his hand to his mouth, licking delicately.

The sound he made was a deep growl, and she felt him widening the splay of her thighs before his rough tongue was parting the lips of her sex and he was drinking directly from her.

Zora mewled as he lapped at her with his fangs pressing into her sensitive flesh. She opened her thighs as wide as she could, tilting her hips in invitation.

As he licked, she rocked her hips against his mouth, and she moaned as he moved faster, voraciously drinking her honey as her body surrendered to his mouth. He gripped her hips and held her as he worked at her with short snarls.

She sobbed and cried out as her channel tried to grip his invading tongue. Her body bucked in his hands as he continued to drink her in.

When she was slumped in his grasp, he moved up her body and settled the engorged head of his cock against her swollen opening. Zora felt a gush of moisture from her body to his, and he slid a few inches into her before pausing again.

Zora opened her eyes and stared up at Regick. Sweat gleamed on his face, shoulders and down his chest. She wanted to run her tongue along his neck, but she couldn't move.

"What do you want, Zora?"

She was flustered. Sex usually didn't involve a lot of requests and answers on her part.

"Um…"

"Just say it."

She mumbled, "I want you close enough to taste you."

He leaned toward her and gave her what she wanted, easing farther inside her as he moved.

She licked at the drops of sweat coating his neck; the taste of him sent her senses reeling. Her hips bucked, taking the column of his cock deep, and she licked him again, shivering as her nipples pebbled and her body shimmied again.

He shuddered as he slid into her, moving as far as he could.

Zora arched her breasts against him, rubbing across the hair on his chest.

Everywhere she touched him, she tingled, until the riot in her senses drove her into a sensual whiteout where all she could do was feel.

His sweat coated her, and he started to move. Regick surrounded her, lowering his body to stroke completely across hers as he thrust into her and withdrew with a deliberately slow motion.

Zora rocked with him, lifting her hips and pulling at the restraints on her wrists. He moved faster, harder and deeper. Zora heard the small cries coming from her throat, but he murmured wordless sounds as he continued to move inside her.

Her senses overloaded, and she bucked as an orgasm ripped through her. Her channel clenched around his, but he kept moving.

Her body kept her at her peak as he stroked in and out. She thrashed against her bonds, but he kept moving at the same insane pace.

She heard herself begging for something, anything, but nothing moved him, he continued to rock inside her, keeping her falling through her climax.

She had to do something, so she lunged up and fastened her teeth to his neck. He shouted and his hips snapped forward, his cock flexed inside her.

The cessation of pleasure was exhausting. Zora let go of Regick's neck and fell back against the pillow. She checked the spot where she had bitten him and didn't see a thing.

Regick leaned forward and pressed his head in the pillow, next to hers. One of his hands reached up, and he released the bands that held her.

She flopped her arms to the sides of her head, and she fought to breathe with the weight of him on her.

Regick shifted, pressing soft kisses against her neck and trailing his tongue

Under His Claw

between her breasts. She muttered and turned her head to one side, her whole body was hypersensitive.

He gripped her jaw and turned her head back to him, kissing her softly.

The extreme gentleness was back, and Zora responded to it. She sighed against his lips and answered his mouth with hers.

Her body had the sexy ache that she had only heard about. Zora could smell blood, but it wasn't a lot. It was, however, definitely hers.

Embarrassed, she turned her head away as he withdrew and rolled free of the bed. She had to use her aching arms to push her thighs together, and when Regick returned, he had a washcloth in his hand, which he pressed to her swollen flesh. The heat made her gasp, but he held it to her as she squirmed.

"Easy, Zora. I got a little enthusiastic. Normally I would lick you clean, but I don't think you are up for it."

She covered her face with her hands while she ignored him, cleaning her of his come and her own.

When he was done, he disappeared to the bathroom again. He lifted her easily in his arms and peeled back the bedding, tucking her in between the sheets.

"Dawn is not too far away, you need your rest. Olvadi will be satisfied."

She felt empty, hollow. He was going to leave her. She was only an opportunity for him. "Thank you for your assistance."

He sighed and crawled into bed next to her. He wrapped her in his arms and held her against the furnace-like heat of his body. "Anytime, Zora. If he demands you do it again, call for me. I will leave my number with your bodyguard."

He pressed a kiss to her temple, and she smiled slightly, giving in to the exhaustion she had so clearly earned.

* * * *

Regick waited until Zora was in deep sleep and the sun was peeking through the tinted glass.

He eased out of bed and got dressed, looking back at her wistfully. He had some research to do, but she might be the one. They had coupled for two hours, and then, she had bitten him. It had been an act of instinct on her part, but it had called an end to their evening. The memory of the feel of her little teeth clamping down on his neck still made him hard.

He tucked his shirt back into his trousers and stroked her dark hair away from her face. Such a tiny body to hold so much power. Olvadi didn't know the half of it.

Regick left Zora's rooms and nodded to the tired vampires on duty. "I am out and she is asleep."

The woman brushed past him and went to check on Zora. When she came back, she pulled him away from the closed door. "You made her bleed."

"I needed to check something, and friction is a brutal force. She has also been without a man for some time. It wasn't much blood, and I am sure she will be fine by morning."

The vampire with the long blonde hair whispered, "I don't want her hurt."

"Neither do I. Take care of her."

The woman nodded, and Regick went off with the sample of Zora's blood in his pocket. If his suspicions were right, Olvadi was about to have a fight on his hands.

* * * *

Zora's legs ached when Olvadi demanded her presence.

Under His Claw

She stood in front of him with her hands folded and her thighs quivering.

"I was going to ask you about your evening, but it seems the night of contact has made its impression on you. Good. You certainly look more relaxed." Olvadi sat with a tiny glass of blood from one of his favourite humans.

She nodded. It was exhaustion and muscle fatigue, but if he wanted to interpret it as satisfaction, he was welcome to.

"Can you do some more work on me today?"

She nodded. "Of course, your majesty."

It was true. Despite her fatigue, she felt energized. She could probably heal more than one ancient wound.

He sipped from his glass, and his ruby red gaze raked over her. "Are you able to do it now?"

She shrugged. "Of course, your majesty."

They went to the private room, and Octavia stood by while the tray with the blade, the towels and the med kit was brought in.

Zora sat in her chair, and she stared in shock as Olvadi opened his trousers and pushed them down. Where his cock should have been was a bundle of scarred tissue.

Olvadi looked down at her. "I became a giant because I was a eunuch; I guarded a seraglio until the day a woman as pale and cool as alabaster was brought to us. I was in love and became her devoted servant, and when she turned me, I swore fealty to her, but it was a love of the mind only. She had cravings, and I could not satisfy them. Eventually, she was destroyed, but I have been content with my position as leader since there was nothing else for me. Now, you have offered me hope, and I pray you do not disappoint me."

She blinked and turned her head. "I need you to lie down for this. I will need to access everything I can, so please completely remove all clothing and lay back on the couch with one leg on the floor and one over the arm."

He arched his dark brow. "You are giving me orders?"

"As your healer. Yes. I can't help you regrow it if I can't get my hands into the proper space."

"Hands, as in both?"

She nodded. "This is not flattery, but this is a two-hand job, much like regrowing a limb."

She turned to Octavia. "It will take over an hour, and he will be sensitive. You will need to bring one of those long silken skirts for him. His body will recover after his next rest cycle."

"Do not speak of me as if I wasn't here."

Zora looked at him in all his scarred and ivory glory. "I know you are here, but you will need to be king the moment I finish this. I will also not be conscious when this is done, so I needed to tell Octavia what you will need. You will be aroused and fascinated by your new equipment. She will need to help you remember who you are and what you are."

He arranged himself as she requested. She brought the tray of items over and took up the disturbing position of kneeling astride Olvadi with her back facing him.

With a grimace, she quickly sliced both her palms and pressed them to the scarred stump. She focused her power on turning her blood into his tissue. His body knew what it should look like. She worked as quickly as she could to make him whole, but it still took her the full hour, and she was exhausted when she

Under His Claw

wiped her blood away from the hard bar of flesh and the sac that hung low and full beneath it.

Her vision blurred and she swayed, falling to the floor, dimly watching Octavia bind her wounds. When Octavia was done, Wilhelm lifted her in his arms and carried her to her rooms.

His cool arms tucked her into her bedding, and he left her alone in the dark.

Zora would have been completely content to fall asleep and stay that way until the following afternoon, but a familiar presence entered her room and placed a hand over her mouth.

She recognized the grip, her scent. She tapped the hand twice. It pulled away from her mouth, and she looked into the glowing golden eyes. She mouthed, "Hi, Grandma."

Zora was amazed it had taken her grandmother this long to find her. She had expected her on day two.

Her grandmother pulled her out of bed and urged her into the hallway. The human corridor was away from all public areas, so that is where Grandma Charani took her.

Grandma was invisible to electronics, and since she had a grip on Zora, so was she.

They ran down the three flights of stairs with all the humans attending to the vampires in the common areas.

It was nerve wracking, but Zora and her grandmother made it out of the vampire building and onto her motorcycle. They roared off into the night with no alarms being raised and no one on their tails.

Zora hung on to her grandmother and hoped no one was punished for her disappearance.

Chapter Five

Charani stopped at a diner and looked at Zora from head to toe. "Why were you dressed?"

Zora sighed, "A vampire tucked me in. They tend to think I get cold easily, so they don't remove my clothing and leave my shoes on."

"It was a man."

"Yup."

Charani sighed. "It figures."

Zora sat with her hands around a cup of coffee; both bandages were now exposed to her grandmother's gaze.

"You have been healing them." Her grandmother's face was disapproving.

"I had to. Alfonso found me and traded my blood for his."

Charani ran her hands through her platinum hair. "How did he know about you?"

"Apparently, there are websites that will lead you to your relatives if you know how to work a search engine. So, he needed me and he found me."

"Are you all right, child?"

"I am. I really am."

"Did they force you?"

She blinked. "The vampires? No."

Her grandmother cracked her spoon in half. "Who did?"

Honesty was always best with her grandmother. She could smell a lie with those senses of hers.

She sat back and smiled at the server who brought her the order of burgers and fries. "It wasn't force, but I was coerced into choosing a lover. He was nice, and he didn't hurt me. He was very careful."

"Who was he?"

Zora cocked her head. "You know, I don't really know. He is a shifter. He told me that much, but aside from his name, I don't know anything about him."

"What was his name?"

Zora ate her fries. "Regick. He had golden hair and golden eyes."

"Any identifying marks?"

"No. Not that I saw."

Charani leaned forward and gripped her hand. "This is important, Zora. Did he draw blood?"

"No. Wait. Yes. Sort of." She blushed.

Her grandmother leaned back. "Damn. Let's hope he isn't looking for you."

"What? Why would he?"

"I need to tell you about your great-great grandmother and the steps she took to protect her children. Your mother should have told you, but she is... well you know."

"Gone."

"Precisely."

Zora sat and listened to the tale of a gypsy princess who fell in love with a nobleman's son and married him. She then listened to the exploit of the gypsy who defended herself and the child she just conceived.

When the daughter was born, Lela took her child to an area known for dragon activity, and she raised her as a lady and introduced her to the local men. Lady Alamina was a hit with the locals, but she fell in love with the seaside. Wandering the ocean daily, she met a water dragon who seduced her and left her with child.

Charani was the next daughter, and she chose a volcanic dragon as a father for her child. Lolli chose a dragon deep in a mine, and Zora was the result.

"Right. I know all that." Zora sipped at her coffee and continued in on her burger.

"So, you know you are the child of three generations of vampire blood and dragons."

"Of course."

"Do you know each of your female ancestors ran and hid from their mates? Alamina was followed by Darcash until she died, and he died when she did. Though they could have simply dropped off the map for privacy. Korlinous still follows me around when I can't dodge him. Right now, he thinks I am in Italy."

"And Mom?"

"She is enjoying a conjugal visit with your father, Yorou, for the last six years. Dragons don't experience time the same way other species do. Oddly enough, the vampire in you causes a peculiar complication. You smell like a human, but your blood tells the tale of your true nature. That was why I asked about your... uh... interaction."

It was good to know Grandma Char was just as uneasy about discussing Zora's sex life as she was.

"Wait, do you mean my father is alive?"

"Yes."

"And my grandfather?"

Charani nodded. "Yup."

"And possibly my great grandfather and grandmother?" Zora pushed her plate to the edge of the table.

"Yes."

"So why have I never met them?"

Her grandmother ran her hand through her hair again. "Dragons are only dragons when they are boys. The girls are carriers, so to speak. The dhampir gene Alamina carried was close enough; it had enough power to allow for a pregnancy."

"Power?"

"Babies born to dragons take a lot of energy to bring to term. Male dragons go their entire lives looking for a woman with the potential to be a mate. That can be a long time to wait for the right woman. They get a little obsessive when they find her."

"Wonderful. Sucks for you. Why are you telling me this?"

Charani rubbed her neck. "Regick has one-twentieth of this continent as his personal territory. You are currently in the centre of it."

Zora swallowed and gulped some water before stammering. "But he... I mean it was just one night."

"It will take him a day or two to get the tests done by a mage. Once he confirms your lineage, there is every chance he will be after you."

"Why are you telling me this?"

"I want to know if you want to run. If you run, I will help you. I will hide you, but you have to decide now."

Zora swayed with exhaustion, and when someone stopped and filled her coffee cup, she looked up and smiled her thanks.

Regick was looking down at her with the coffee pot in his hand. "You are welcome."

She spoke to her grandmother while staring at Regick. "I think we are too late."

He smiled politely and handed the coffeepot to the star-struck waitress. "Thank you, Sara."

"No problem." She whisked the coffeepot away.

Zora looked at him and cocked her head. "I think she is going to bronze it."

He shrugged. "May I join you?"

Charani's face was oscillating between amused and irritated. "Please."

Zora moved over, and he settled in next to her, his thigh pressed to hers.

Under His Claw

Her grandmother looked him over. "You cover up fairly well."

Zora looked at him in surprise. "What is he covering up?"

"Your friend is referring to my appearance. This is a glamour which makes me acceptable to humans."

"I am sorry. Regick, this is my grandmother, Charani. Charani, this is Regick."

He extended his hand to Charani, and he jolted slightly as she took it. "You truly are her grandmother. That does explain a few things."

Charani sighed, "It seems you have a few things to discuss with Zora. Does the vampire know she is gone?"

Regick nodded. "He has search parties out for her, but he is looking for a vampire or a shifter, not your grandmother."

Zora made a face. "I hope no one is in trouble because of me."

Charani leaned forward and took her hand. "Sweetie, you were kidnapped and enslaved. If they can survive the damage, they can recover from it, and no shifters will be harmed. It is against the treaty."

"It isn't the shifters I am worried about. The king's personal guard have been very kind to me."

Regick sighed. "I suppose I will have to get you somewhere safe and then invite Olvadi over for a conversation."

She was nervous. "What do you mean, get me somewhere safe?"

"He means he is going to bring you into his lair and keep you there until you give in to him." Charani scowled and leaned back.

Regick raised his brows. "Hardly a lair. My home is well appointed and very secure. She will be safe there until we negotiate a settlement. There is even a shopping centre on the premises. You can get some more comfortable clothing."

She looked down at her rumpled designer suit. "This suit was fine."

"And uncomfortable. It showed in every move you made."

Zora frowned. "You only saw me the one time, at the party and then... after."

"Olvadi sent me your picture to lure me to the party. You were wearing a blue suit and heels which were half a size too small for you." He smiled.

Charani snorted. "Dragons have an excellent style sense."

"So, you told her what I am."

"I did."

"You are a dragon's mate."

Charani frowned. "I am."

"Where is he?"

"On a wild goose chase. I find I get along best with my mate if we are in different cities."

"Who is he?"

Zora's grandmother laughed, "Oh, no. You will call him, and then, the next thing I know, he will be flying me out to some chunk of rock for negotiations."

Zora frowned at the second reference to negotiations. "What does that mean?"

Her grandmother smiled at her. "Sex, dear."

Sure, Charani didn't look a day over thirty-five, but her air of wisdom seemed to have always been there. The idea of her grandmother having sex should have been normal, but for some reason, it freaked Zora out.

Her grandmother decided for her. "Get her safe. If he is looking already, we don't have the time I thought we did."

"I would like to ensure your safety as well."

Charani smiled. "I have faith in Zora's ability to handle you. I need to get back on the road and destroy my trail. Zee-zee, I give you permission to tell him our

Under His Claw

family secrets. He will learn them soon enough anyway."

Her grandmother disappeared from the table and the bike fired up outside, she spun in a circle and headed for the open road.

Regick looked at Zora with an amused expression. "Does she do that a lot?"

"Often enough." She looked around and made a face. "And she skipped out on the check, and I don't have enough to pay the bill."

He grinned and took her wrist, snapping the bangles off her left wrist and then the right. He left them on the table and said, "That should cover it."

She blinked. "That should."

Regick rose to his feet and held out his hand. "If you want to hide, we need to leave now. The vampires are getting closer. You have been careless enough with your blood that they are all in search of it."

Zora took his hand, and she tried to ignore the excitement of her body at his smallest touch.

They exited the diner and a dark limo pulled up. Regick tucked her inside and followed after. The door closed and the car glided forward.

"Home, Fred."

The silhouette behind the privacy glass nodded, and they turned back to the city.

Zora shivered.

Regick moved next to her and pulled her into his lap, cuddling her into his warmth. He pressed a kiss to her temple and inhaled deeply. "I can't believe I didn't sense this before."

"Sense what?"

"You are a blend of dragon and vampire which has never walked the earth before. It is a very good thing and will make it difficult for Olvadi to put a claim on you."

Under His Claw

"Why?"

"Because, by the Natural Resources Treaty of 1905, no dragon can be held, chained, threatened or enslaved by any agency, supernatural or human. It disrupts the balance of nature to hold a dragon out of their territory. You have at least one dragon in your bloodline, so it puts you under our protection."

"Three."

"What?"

"Three dragons. Water, fire and earth. Each of my ancestresses since Lela and Alfonso has been a dragon's mate. I didn't know they were still all involved."

"When dragons mate, it is for life, and the life of our partner matches our own. If we have learned anything over the years, it is no dragon has been lucky enough to find an easy mate. If we don't fight for our own partners, we don't keep them."

Zora smiled at the thought. "You

might be the first bored dragon on record. I am hardly what one would call feisty."

"Perhaps you need the chance to stand up for yourself and be what you were meant to be."

Chapter Six

She got her own room and a bed large enough for four. Stripping, she crawled between the sheets and dozed off. She was so damned tired.

* * * *

"Where is my property, Regick?"

Olvadi was in a foul humour. His guards were cowed and huddling in on themselves.

"Ah, yes. Your property. You forced her to seek out a sex partner, and as I was by far the superior specimen, she chose me." Regick didn't agree with the idea of thrones, but his employees were nearby and at attention. They were seated at the boardroom table where he engaged in all of his more trying transactions.

"And yet you left her and walked out of my home."

Olvadi seemed different, more hostile. His normally calm demeanour looked like it could shatter at any moment.

"There is a matter you and I are going to have to discuss."

"Give her back and we will discuss it."

"That is what must be discussed. We will not give to the vampires that which belongs to the dragons."

Olvadi shook the room with his bellow. "What?"

"She is of my kind. Three dragons are in her immediate lineage, and this trumps her dhampir beginning."

The king clawed at the table. "You do

not understand. She has value to the vampire community."

"Does she know about his value?"

"She does."

"She didn't mention it. What is the nature of the value?"

The vampire king leaned forward. "I am not comfortable mentioning it."

"Then, you will not see her. You know as well as I do that my claim trumps yours tenfold."

"You don't understand."

"Then explain it to me. We have been friends for a long time. She will be my mate. You will not get to her unless it is through me."

Olvadi gritted his teeth. "Fine. She heals vampires. She can use her blood to remove damage left by torture in our previous lives and silver and holy-water inflicted damage from after we changed."

"She can do all that?" He was impressed.

"Yes. She even regrew my genitals the day before she disappeared."

Regick sat straight. "My mate regrew your cock?"

Olvadi looked nervous; his crimson eyes were banked. "She did, at my order."

"Then, you have taken all you will from my mate. If you wish her services, you will come to me and negotiate a proper fee for her skills. Threatening her life is not acceptable."

The vampire king drummed his fingers on the table. "I had thought to complete my healing and take her as my bride."

Regick felt his glamour slip with his flash of irritation. "No."

Olvadi leaned back. "Take it easy, my friend. If you have claimed her, it is enough. We have known each other for centuries."

Under His Claw

Regick calmed himself, and he set his mind to negotiation. "What will you offer for another healing?"

"Will you keep her ability to heal vampires as our secret?"

Regick noted his friend was very nervous. There was a reason for it; if word of the repairs got out before Zora got settled into her power, she would be vulnerable. That wasn't something he wanted.

"She will remain as my mate, and you will come to visit with your entourage as a caring former employer. Now, what are you willing to offer?"

They settled down into the business of negotiating for her services, and Olvadi put businesses down on the table and Regick began to realize what a potential gold mine was sleeping upstairs.

Six months of healing services created a very nice portfolio for Zora. Regick hoped she would appreciate his decisions.

When the paperwork had been drawn up and signed, Olvadi smiled, "You will be getting rich off Zora's efforts."

"You didn't read the name on the transfer of ownership. These are all going to be Zora's. It is her blood going into the work, she should benefit."

Olvadi looked confused.

Regick finished up the paperwork and handed it to his lawyer. The gargoyle nodded and took the sheaf of papers off to his office. "They will be filed immediately."

Olvadi nodded. "Of course. Now, why put the businesses in Zora's name?"

"So she has a reason to stay." He didn't mention no dragon's mate would remain in one place unless she could build a nest. That was none of the vampire's business. He would not make the mistake that the others had made with her ancestors. If she needed reasons to stay with him, he would give them to her.

* * * *

Zora sat up suddenly, her heart pounding at the shock of unfamiliar surroundings.

She clutched the sheets to her chest and stared at the door in fear, but no one came in.

"Maybe I just went to a hotel and got drunk and passed out."

The carpet felt thick and soft under her feet as she crossed the room to look out the windows. The room was decorated in a subtle combination of soft gold and cream. It was light, bright and huge. The window looked out over the city of Arbor, and based on the height of the window, she was in the Scale, the tallest building for two states.

She could see a full one hundred

eighty degrees; the window was arched in a curved bubble from floor to ceiling. Zora didn't know how she could have such an expensive hotel room; she didn't even know the Scale had hotel rooms.

A quiet knock on the door made her check to make sure she was tightly wrapped in the sheet before she turned. "Come in."

A young woman came in with a tray balanced on one arm. "Good day, Miss Zora."

"Um, good day."

"I am Leah Marx, and I will be your personal assistant if you have no objections."

The tray was set on the dark and slickly polished bleached-oak table. Leah removed the cover on the tray, and the smell of bacon and other treats wafted to Zora.

"Why would I need a personal assistant?"

Under His Claw

"If you accept me for the moment, I will tell you."

"Consider yourself hired."

Leah grinned, sat at the table and told Zora about everything which had gone on while she slept.

The most interesting thing to Zora was that Leah and her family had been in Regick's employ for centuries. Gargoyles were notoriously long lived and not prey for vampires. It made them excellent employees for dragons.

The second most interesting thing was Zora now owned a hair and nail salon as well as three boutiques.

"So, Regick demanded it and Olvadi gave in?"

Leah shrugged. "I have worked for him all my life, and when Regick makes up his mind about something, he gets what he wants. Anyway, my father is his lawyer and my mother is his accountant. They have all the details."

Zora fidgeted. "So, can I go out?"

"Of course. I will take you to your appointments and act as your driver and bodyguard, but you can go anywhere you like, see anyone you want."

"As long as I take you with me."

"I can literally blend in with my surroundings. It will be like I am not there." Leah went invisible right in front of Zora's eyes.

"That is a nice trick."

She reappeared. "We try to be more subtle than the vampires, but the result is the same; you will be protected."

"What am I being protected from?"

Leah smirked, "For the first few months, female shifters who wanted Regick for their own will be after you. For today, I am going to get you some clothing and you will attend your meeting with the mayor and the governor."

"What?"

"Regick is one of the largest landowners in his territory, and he also owns all of the natural resources. Becoming his mate will make you exceptionally wealthy and a public personality."

Zora sank back. "That is not the career path I had for myself."

"You had a plan?"

"I was going to remain obscure and go from small job to small job until I figured out what I wanted to do next. My life was an endless stream of not attracting attention."

"And now, here you are." Leah's hands took in the expanse of the room.

"Right. With nothing to wear. What happened to my clothes?"

"I am pretty sure Regick burned them. Nothing from the vampire's court is allowed to remain here."

"Where does it leave me?"

"It leaves you as the bride of the great golden dragon. Now, you finish eating while I get your clothing." Leah patted her on the arm and was out of the room in a heartbeat.

Zora settled in and poured a cup of coffee before working her way through her fruit cup.

She took a shower and was finger combing her hair when a knock sounded again. "Come in, Leah."

"I am not Leah. How are you feeling?" Regick came in and leaned against the window.

Zora tightened the towel and checked to make sure only a little thigh was showing. The towel covered her to barely above her knees. "Um, fine. I thought you were Leah."

He grinned, and the sunlight glinted off his hair. "I get that a lot."

She giggled.

"So, has Leah briefed you?"

Zora took in the heat in his gaze, and she pulled her hair forward and kept finger combing it. "She did."

"So, you do not need to worry about Olvadi. I have arranged for you to continue healing the vampires he brings to you because you seem to want to heal them."

"You caught on to it?"

"You have an instinct to take care of those in your immediate vicinity. If you want to forge strong links to the local community, it is your prerogative. I will simply keep you safe while you do it."

She sucked in a deep breath and blurted out the question on her mind. "What do you want from me?"

"I want you as my mate, and I want you to do it voluntarily. If we were humans, I would begin courtship, but we are not, and this is the way our people do things. An acceptable mate is kept separated from all other dragons while the male attempts to seduce her into bearing his young."

Zora chuckled, "And at that point, he

relaxes his guard."

"Which is how your ancestresses got away. I want you to want to stay with me because you choose to."

She swallowed. He had started to move closer, and she tensed nervously. He took her hand and pulled her upright, and she was reminded precisely how large he actually was.

Regick put his index finger under her chin, and when she looked up at him, his kiss warmed her from the inside out. He breathed a sensual fire through her, which left her aching. Zora swayed toward him until her towel brushed against his shirt.

The heat in him attracted her in a way no human male's ever had. She had never considered that she was technically a dragon by birth, but it would explain a lot.

She was unsure of her next step, but she slid her fingers into his hair and

Under His Claw

pulled his head back. "What is your glamour, and can I see you without it?"

He shuddered, and she got the impression that she had talked dirty to him.

"Not this afternoon. We will revisit the discussion tonight. Leah is waiting outside, and your first introduction as my mate will occur in thirty minutes. As much as I would like to continue this, and I really would like to continue this..."

She could feel his claws trailing against her cheek.

"It is time for you to get dressed. Leah!"

The door opened, and Leah came in, her arms loaded with bags. "Regick, please leave. I have work to do, and we are running out of time."

He sighed, kissed Zora softly and strode out of the room.

Leah kicked the door closed behind

him and said, "All right, strip. We don't have much time."

Public nudity was something she was getting used to, so she dropped the towel and let the gargoyle dress her. She had a meeting with the mayor to get to, after all.

Chapter Seven

There was something to be said for gargoyle fashion sense. Zora was wearing a flowing skirt in deep blue chiffon and a long blazer, which fell to mid-thigh. Her shoes were three-inch heels, and her hair was arranged up over her ears in elegant twists and fell straight back to her shoulders. Regick sat next to her at the meeting, and she stayed close to him during the cocktail hour after the charity ball had been arranged.

"Do you do a lot of this sort of thing?" Zora looked up at him through her lashes.

"Quite a bit. I have more riches than I

could spend in a thousand human lifetimes. If the folks around me are more comfortable and feel cared for, they work harder and are more willing to risk their lives in the defense of my property. It is a very bald manipulation, but it has worked well for the last few hundred years." He shrugged.

Zora chuckled. "I will translate it as you want the people around you to be happy and ignore the rest."

He slid his arm around her waist, and he smiled. "Looking for the good in people. It is an endearing quality."

"You don't?"

"I do my research. I know about what happened when you were a child."

She paused as she sipped at her glass of water. "Wow. You said that right here in the middle of this little gathering."

"I thought it was clever of me to keep things from getting emotional. You were kidnapped?"

Under His Claw

"And my blood was used to repair other vampires. When my mom caught up to us, she burned the entire nest to the ground, and we went on the run. It echoed other family experiences a little too closely, she got angry." She tried to keep a smile on her face as the others on the charity committee glanced their way.

"And yet, you still feel for vampires."

"I do. They were human once, and they still feel pain and humiliation. Sure, they are arrogant and vain, but they still have feelings. A little kindness helps them remember that."

"Or they take it as weakness."

She shrugged and sipped at her water again. "I can give and I can take away."

Regick was startled. "What?"

"The building blocks come from my body. I can heal the damage or I can return it to the original state I found it in."

"I think we need to discuss this in private."

She smiled brightly at him and blew him a kiss. "You uncorked the bottle. Are you upset with what came out?"

He tightened his grip on her waist. "No, but like myself, I believe you are far more than meets the eye."

She wrapped her arm around him, picked his pocket and showed him his wallet. "You could say that."

He tucked the wallet back in his pocket. "Something else to discuss."

"The tip of the iceberg."

The governor came up and wanted to discuss his policies on shifter work-employment regulations. After all, it wasn't fair the best jobs went to the strongest shifters while the others had to pick up the dregs.

She was eased away from Regick, and it would have caused her to panic, but she could see Leah behind her in the background as silent backup.

She spoke with the governor's wife,

Under His Claw

and the woman was looking at her with envy.

"So, Regick is your mate?"

Zora nodded politely. "He is."

"We didn't know he was seeing someone."

Zora sipped at her water again. "Neither did I."

"But, you must have been seeing each other."

"Oh, yes. I have seen all of him." She smiled brightly as the other woman got frustrated. The gossip wasn't forthcoming, and the woman was starving for it.

Leah eased toward her. "Miss Zora, You have an appointment."

The governor's wife sneered at her, "Do you mind? We were having a conversation."

Zora's blood rose in irritation. "I am coming with you, Leah. Thank you for the reminder. Madam, speak to Leah like that again and you will never speak to me. Are we clear?"

It was a weird threat, but the woman paled. Zora left with Leah and breathed a sigh of relief when they were out of the cocktail party.

"Thank you. Do I really have an appointment?"

"Yes, Regick wishes to speak with you. He could not extricate himself any other way, so now that you are out of the room, he will simply follow you by claiming the undeniable hormones of the newly mated."

Zora blushed as they headed for the elevator. "Will it work as a social excuse?"

"With less than a hundred dragons on the earth, there are few, if any, records of their mating habits. It is considered best to get out of the way of a dragon with sex on his mind."

"That would be sound thinking."

Leah grinned. "And yet, it is the last

Under His Claw

thing that you did."

"It wasn't really a choice. When you are a woman alone with no physical defenses, you have to choose your battles. When it came to Regick, there was no choice. All the other shifters ran away the moment he walked in the door."

They went up to the penthouse on the fortieth floor, and Leah waited in the elevator. "He will be up in a moment. Have a nice evening. See you tomorrow."

She waved politely, and the door to the elevator closed.

Zora turned, and she looked at her surroundings. The large recreational space was neatly arranged, and as she went exploring, she found a guest bathroom and the kitchen. The refrigerator was sparsely filled, but it contained her favourite soda and a cupboard disgorged her ideal snack foods.

She poured some in a bowl, put a chip

clip on the bag and wandered into the bedroom, where her hands nearly dropped the bowl. The bed was huge, the window beyond led onto a rooftop large enough to land a small aircraft, but it was the arrangement of cuffs and straps on the bed which made her flinch.

She steeled her nerves and crossed the room, touching one of the straps and ignoring the flare of heat in her belly. Before she could get too involved in her examination, she opened the door and walked out onto the rooftop, noting the scarred tarmac and scorch marks.

Zora wandered to the edge of the roof and climbed up on a low wall, dangling her legs over the edge. The wind tugged at her hair and ruffled her skirt as she ate her chips. It was a striking view as far as she could see. The distant mountains would mark the edge of one part of Regick's territory. She kicked her feet and wondered how much she would en-

Under His Claw

joy this if she were one of those people afraid of heights. It was a fear she had never understood.

She crunched at the chips and watched the sun redden in the sky.

"I wondered where you had gotten to." Regick sat next to her on the low wall.

She offered him the chips, and he accepted, crunching while the wind swirled around them.

"So, how often do you use that bondage equipment?"

He coughed. "It was supposed to be removed this afternoon, and you were supposed to be in your own quarters."

"I am guessing that Leah wants me informed."

"I use them when I have sex with other shapeshifters. If you don't bind them, they can change when things get interesting. I have not used it in months, but it is kept in ready condition."

"So you were having it removed?"

"I can subdue my own mate without the use of physical restraints."

"Cocky."

"Thank you for noticing." He grinned.

She set the empty bowl down behind them and licked her fingers. He took her hand in his and sucked her fingers, one by one. As he sucked, she felt a low tugging in her sex.

"Why would you want a mate who couldn't change shape? Isn't that like... half a mate?"

He smiled while licking at her palm. "You know why dragons are attracted to the damsels?"

"Not a clue."

"Usually, the villagers staked out the most independent, the bravest and the most intelligent women because their men were weak. Dragons know a good woman when they see it, and they don't pass up the chance at happiness."

Under His Claw

"So, what you are saying is because these women were mouthy, they got sacrificed?"

He trailed his tongue down the edge of her wrist before he moved closer and kissed her neck. "They were sacrificed over and over again. Many lived good lives with their dragon mates, but others left the dragon with enough treasure to start a new life far away."

"With their children?"

"Dragons don't let their children go."

She tilted her head so he could trail the licks and kisses down her neck. "They do in my family."

"That will be a discussion for a different day. I believe you wanted to know what I looked like without my glamour."

She shivered. He was trailing his hand between her breasts and undoing the jacket as he went.

"I do."

"I don't want to frighten you."

Her jacket opened, and the wind cooled her skin as his hand warmed it. "It takes a lot to frighten me."

The hand on her breast scaled over, and the scales spread up his arm, under his shirt and over his face, enhancing the sharp blades of his cheekbones and the cut of his jawline with a ridge of spines extending across his temples into his hairline.

His neck thickened to ridiculous proportions, and his chest and shoulders widened. The wings, which became apparent, were huge and large enough to support the massive humanoid body they were attached to.

Zora smiled and cupped his jaw, pulling his head to hers. "Still not scared."

His lips curved against hers, and he wrapped his arms around her, pushing them both off the rooftop.

Zora held tight to him as he slowly spiralled around his building, watching the world go by over his shoulder. When he pulled her down into his arms, she looked into his golden eyes and he kissed her.

His wings began to pump hard, and they rose slowly, back to the rooftop where they had started.

He landed near the doorway and ducked his head as he entered his bedroom. He slid the door closed and settled her at the edge of the bed, kneeling in front of her.

"You are really not afraid?"

She grinned. "You are a dragon. This is what you look like. I am a mutt. This is what I look like."

"You are not a mutt. You are the product of your ancestresses wanting the best for their daughters. Daughters who did the same as their mothers."

"They sought means to have their children survive. They had no idea that they would bear daughters." She stroked his scaled skin, enjoying the press of it against her fingers and palms.

His fangs showed as he smiled, "I would not mind a daughter."

She sighed, "Let's not discuss things that will probably never happen."

His eyes grew hot. She could almost feel the heat radiating off his gaze. His fingers worked at the front clasp of her bra for a moment before he hooked his claws under it and simply sliced it free.

He pressed his face between her breasts, and he exhaled against her skin. The heat spiralled through her, and she swayed with her head back and her hands clenched on the bedding. He pulled her jacket off before lifting her feet and flipping her shoes away. Her skirt fought him, and it did not win.

The wisp of panties she had been wearing was not designed to deal with claws. He flicked away the shreds and buried his face between her thighs.

His tongue stroked at her, licking the wet honey before she gasped. His tongue thrust into her and undulated inside.

She twisted at the rough sensation of his scales against her inner thighs and screeched when he stroked her clit with a hard twist of his thumb. The subtle foreplay of the flight had gotten her blood pounding, and it was a short trip from panic to orgasm.

She shrieked, Regick backed away, throwing away the too-tight clothing and showing her his shoulders were not the only thing that had gotten wider.

His cock now sported ridges down its length, and its width had increased by enough to make her really doubt that he was going to fit.

Chapter Eight

With both of them naked, he stepped toward her, and it took all her nerve not to run for it. He knelt again, lifted her by cupping her ass, and her thighs were draped over his shoulders.

Regick thrust his tongue into her, and she could feel it thicken as he stroked it in and out. The smooth slickness was a tease, and she gripped his hair to hold him in place.

He easily pulled away from her, and to her embarrassment, he licked his hand over and over before wrapping his hand around his cock and stroking the saliva over it.

Under His Claw

Without a word, he kissed her, flipped her around, and he positioned her into a hands-and-knees position on the edge of the bed. It put her at the perfect height for him.

She braced herself as his cock wedged into her, but her tension wouldn't allow him in any further.

She heard him licking something again, and to her shock, he pressed his finger against her ass. She gasped, but his cock slid in an inch further. He pressed again, and she allowed his cock in another inch.

She squirmed, mewled and rocked forward, but he caught her around the waist with his free hand, and his finger continued its devastating entry. Mercifully, no claw was apparent.

The burn in her ass eased suddenly, and his cock settled with his thighs pressing against hers.

She felt full, extremely full, but when

he started to move inside her, she lost track of thought and concentrated on feeling.

Her breasts swayed as he thrust into her and retreated before surging forward again. She braced herself on the sheets as the sunlight painted the bed red. Her breathing took on a ragged pattern; she moaned when he thrust in and gasped when he pulled back. Zora was rocked over and over until she was sure her body couldn't contain the pleasure anymore, and still, she climbed higher.

His clawed hand cupped her breasts and stroked them as he drove into her with more speed and muttering in a deep, dark voice and a language she didn't understand.

She was trapped with her body on fire and her blood pounding in her ears. When she felt more pressure in her ass, she mewled but he withdrew his finger. As two fingers pressed into her, she screamed and her body bucked hard against him. It was pulling at him and goading him into a flurry of thrusts, which culminated in him pressing his lips to the back of her neck and pressing his teeth in while his hips jerked into hers.

Zora sobbed and dropped until her forehead was pressed to the sheets. Her body felt raw, and her ass throbbed with short pulses. He withdrew his fingers, and she shivered at the loss.

Regick pulled free of her, and as she rolled to her side, she watched him exhale fire over his hand, burning off all traces of its recent activity.

His hand was still hot when he tucked her under the comforter and he slid in next to her, wearing his glamour.

He chuckled. "You handled that well."

She sighed and wiped at her tears. "Thanks, it was just..."

"A little much. I apologize, but you

were too tight for me to work myself in without surprising you, and your ass is so darned cute." He kissed her shoulder.

She swallowed and was definitely glad it had only been his fingers.

His hands stroked over her breasts and belly, and she had to admit it was soothing.

"Are you in the mood to talk, Zora?"

She nodded. "Sure. I am getting my mental footing back."

"Good. What do you mean that you can undo the vampire's healing?"

"Simply what I said. No vampire can regrow tissue. The healing I have administered so far has been ancient damage. If I were so inclined, I could remove my tissue from their body, and they would be left open and bleeding just as they were on the day of the original damage."

"So, you basically own every vampire you have ever healed."

"Well, my mother took care of most of

them. She could access her father's fire or so Grandma always told me."

Zora turned in his arms and burrowed against his chest. He wrapped his arms around her and cuddled her close.

"Any more questions?"

"Who is your father?"

"Yorou."

"He who dwells in darkness?"

She shrugged. "I don't know. I have never met him."

She suddenly realized, "Do all dragons have weird names?"

He shrugged. "We get references to our major traits."

"What is your dragon name?"

He mumbled against her hair. "Regick, he who gilds the skies."

"Nice. Is it on your business cards?"

He smacked her butt. "Funny."

She sighed. "What else do you want to know?"

"What other dragons are in your lineage?"

"Darcash and Korlinous. My great grandfather and grandfather respectively."

He whistled low. "Impressive."

"What are their other names?"

"Darcash is he who commands the waves, and Korlinous is he who bathes in fire."

"Nice. Water, fire, earth and now air. It is a funny lineage."

She thought about a child descended from four generations of dragons and four different elements. Grounding it would be a problem, and who would that child consider as a mate?

"Would you like to see them?"

"See who?"

"Your male ancestors. The dragons are all connected, and I can make a few calls."

"What would happen to us if my father came for a visit?"

Under His Claw

"Nothing. You are mine. He might offer a dowry, but I don't need it." He chuckled.

"Why would you invite them?"

"In a word, etiquette. I have mated with their bloodline and they need to know me. If they need anything, they will know I will be there at their call."

She thought about it. She had always wanted to know her father, and her mother had never said anything bad about him. "Sure. Yes. You can contact them."

"Good. I will contact all three of them."

"Wait. Isn't Darcash dead?"

"No. He is still in the great North Sea with his mate. Why?"

"Grandmother thought that her mother was dead already."

"Ah. Awkward. We will see what there is to be seen when and if they return my call."

"They might not?"

"They might not. We have a society, but we don't socialize much. It will depend on them."

She sighed and cuddled against him. It wasn't even three minutes later her stomach growled, and she cursed her metabolism. "I need to find some dinner."

"There is a restaurant downstairs if you like."

"Do they serve burgers?"

"They can." He rubbed his chin against her head.

"Then, I need a shower and some clothing."

"Clothing we will have to get in your room, but the shower, I can arrange here."

There was a strange anticipation in him as he rolled to his feet with her in his arms. He stood her up on the tile and whistled softly; a cascade of glittery fire splashed against her and cleared her skin of sweat and other fluids. He whistled up, down and bent to clean between her thighs. The fire splashed and disappeared as it touched her, taking away dirt and oils and leaving a warm tingles from head to toe.

"Now, do we sacrifice your sheets or make a sprint for the elevator to get me clothing."

He smirked, "Or we can take the stairs."

"Stairs?"

"Of course. I will never be inaccessible to you, even if you do not wish to share my bed."

She chuckled. "That is a possibility?"

"Of course. No couple wishes to spend every night together, not when you live as long as we shall. You might need to work late or I might. You will need your own library and your own offices. The apartment below can serve as both."

"Show me."

He led her past the master bathroom and to a blank wall behind it. He pressed the wall, and it slid back. He took her hand and led her down a spiral staircase to the room she had occupied previously.

"Wait. Where is the bed?"

He looked up at the ceiling. "Upstairs."

"What about no couple always sleeping together?"

"I lied. I will be next to you, under you or within you for the first century or so."

"What if I don't live that long?"

"You will, or I will rip the guts out of the person who killed you before I follow you into the afterlife."

She made a face and found the wardrobe. It was sparse, but she found replacement underwear and a simple black dress. She slipped on a pair of sensible heels, and she put her hands on her hips. "All right. I am ready for dinner, and you are still naked. Get dressed and bring your wallet. I don't have money yet."

"Fair enough. May I bring my phone?"

"Of course. Your life doesn't stop just because mine hasn't started."

He shook his head and sprinted up the spiral staircase, returning in two minutes wearing a tight T-shirt and jeans.

The simple girl in her soul sighed at the picture his muscles made in the shirt. It was tight enough to define everything with enough room to make it look like he wasn't trying too hard.

"Those jeans are pretty tight. Is your wallet in there?"

He crossed his arms and narrowed his eyes at her in disapproval. "You are cruising for a spanking."

Since she was pretty sure he had paddles readily available, she put her hands up. "You are right. I am sorry. I should know better than to give you a sarcastic compliment."

He closed his eyes for a moment, and when he opened them again, he was smiling. He turned around. "Look all you like. Yes, I brought my wallet."

She admired his butt and walked over to pat it. He whipped around and caught her in his arms.

"Having a mate is new to me as well. I may say foolish things from time to time."

"I will probably forgive you. That's in my nature, well as long as the spanking doesn't become a reality. I am not a fan of pain, even at playtime."

He nodded against her temple. "Noted, though I may try and change your mind now and then."

She inhaled his warm and comforting scent. "Fine, now let's get me that burger."

"As my lady commands."

Chapter Nine

The spa on the third floor had a private room, and it was there she healed Olvadi.

She smiled at the vampire king as he settled on the massage table with his back facing her. "So, your majesty, how is your new junk treating you?"

"It responds quite well. I have had eight lovers of both sexes, and they all appear pleased with the results."

Zora blinked and pierced her hands before slathering her blood over his back and moving up and down the whip scars in even passes.

"You are using a different technique

today."

"This is a different type of scar. The stroke of the whip moved across you evenly so that is how it will be healed."

She kept making the passes, and she could feel the damage breaking apart and her blood smoothing the skin.

"Are you content with Regick?"

Zora smiled. "I am relatively free here, which is refreshing. Even living in Orchard, I had a hard time making ends meet and wasn't able to make many friends. I am beginning a new life."

"And all you have to do is sleep with a dragon."

"It has been done before in my family."

She felt the tension in him.

"What?"

"Your majesty, do not pretend you do not know of my lineage. I am well aware Regick told you when he negotiated the fees for my services."

He exhaled, though, strictly speaking, he didn't need to breathe.

"Octavia misses you."

"I miss her as well. If you wish to use my services beyond the next six months, you may consider trading her to me for repairs to those holy-water gouges in your thighs or re-growing Tarthos's arm."

Her hands continued their relentless sweep with the blood sliding under them.

"I do not wish to part with Octavia. She is one of my favoured lovers."

Zora made a face. Octavia's preferences ran to women. She had slept with men, but it wasn't what she wanted. If she was one of Olvadi's favourite lovers, Zora bet the sentiment wasn't returned.

Another ten minutes passed and she finished the repair. The towels waiting for her were warm and damp. They helped her remove her blood from Olvadi and assisted her in stopping the flow from her hands.

"You are done, your majesty. Next appointment is in one week."

He sat up and his ruby eyes glared at her. "Only one a week? That was not the deal."

"I have read the contract. There was nothing in there about frequency of treatments, only six months of treatments were mentioned. I was to decide the schedule, and since I am now involved in the local community, it is important for me to pace myself. Healing takes a lot out of me, and if Regick and I are to have a family, I need to conserve my energy."

"You are pregnant?"

She shrugged. "Perhaps yes, perhaps no. Not for lack of trying."

Olvadi checked out his now blemish-free back in the mirror. "You do do excellent work."

She nodded. "I am aware of it. I am going to summon my assistant. She will help me with the bandages."

"I could help you."

"She has requested I ask for her help. She has been charged with my health and well-being, and she does a wonderful job."

She used her elbow to press a button in the wall, and Leah's subtle knock came a moment later. She sat Zora down on a spa chair and leaned in to lick Zora's wounds. After she applied the saliva, she wrapped Zora's hand with gauze to protect it.

Olvadi shrugged into his shirt. "Gargoyles."

There was such distaste in his tone that she looked over her shoulder with an admonishing glare. "My house, my rules, your majesty. Manners matter."

He nodded and stalked from the room, closing the door with a solid click.

Under His Claw

"You should not have done that. He will be angry."

"His dick works now. He is angry twenty-three hours per day."

Leah was startled into laughing. It took a bit of effort to make her smile, and Zora enjoyed the sound."

When she was all done, Leah fired up the small brazier and they burned all blood-smeared items. It was time that Zora took what was in her veins more seriously.

"How did the session go tonight?" Regick smiled at her over the steak dinner he had ordered.

After spending the night with her own blood, Zora was having fish.

"It was pretty good. He needs about seven more treatments to give himself the flawless body he has always wanted. I am worried about Octavia though. I think I will have to make some moves on getting possession of her. Can we do that?"

"What? Have a vampire on the payroll? Sure. It would have to be done with Olvadi's agreement, or we would have to move her to another city and get their king to agree to let us have her. They are like leashed dogs. They have to be licensed and monitored wherever they go. If they are not, they breed out of control."

"Breeding is a funny word."

"Speaking of breeding, how are we doing?" He waggled his eyebrows.

She laughed. "How would I know? This is not something I can consult a regular physician for."

"Perhaps your grandmother could tell you."

"Perhaps she could, but she isn't here."

"She arrives tomorrow, as does your grandfather. They have agreed to a reconciliation." He beamed.

"Wow. She has been avoiding him as long as I have been alive. This will be interesting."

He shrugged. "Since he will be landing on the roof, I thought it would be a good idea to take the gear out of the bedroom. I don't want it that interesting."

She snickered and finished her cod. "Too bad, I was working up the nerve to let you try more than spread-eagling me to the bed."

His fork bent sharply. He gave her a narrow-eyed look. "Don't tease."

"We are in public. It is all I have." She drank water and smirked.

The restaurant on the third floor was open, charming and owned by the man across from her. Regick was an excellent landlord and restaurateur. The clientele was having a good time, and the arrangements made each table a private oasis. Of course, they were sitting at the owner's table, so it was the best seat in the house.

Their server came by and whisked her plate away the moment she finished it. They were very efficient without a lot of chitchat.

She flipped through the dessert menu, and the manager came over and whispered in Regick's ear. Her mate sat up and started to straighten his clothing.

"Bring them in."

She decided on the crème brulee and was putting her menu down when a couple approached them. Regick got to his feet and greeted the other man. The blonde woman was staring at Zora with the same shape and shade of amber eyes that she saw when she looked at her grandmother.

The face was that of her grandmother as well but the colouring was wrong. The man's hair was a blue so dark, it was

Under His Claw

nearly black. His ears were slightly pointed, and they were pierced in six places down each curve.

"Alamina." Zora breathed the word.

Alamina smiled. "Tsura. You are lovelier than I imagined."

"I thought you had passed on."

"It is hard to die when you are wed to a dragon. You stay around as long as they do."

Zora got to her feet and ran over to hug her great grandmother. "I am glad you are here."

Alamina finally pried her off, laughing and wiping at tears. Her mate was standing next to her, exasperated.

"Tsura, this is your great grandfather and the first dragon in your bloodline, Darcash."

She extended her hand to him. "I am pleased to meet you, Darcash."

He smiled and took her hand. "May I have a hug?"

She cautiously moved toward him and embraced him. He squeezed her, and she heard him inhale in a long draw.

When they separated, he nodded to Alamina. "Definitely our blood."

Regick laughed. "With this family's penchant for running, you are definitely due your doubt."

They had a moment and the men chortled.

Zora asked her great grandmother, "Are you hungry? I was just about to order dessert, but if you would like dinner, I could keep you company."

Regick nodded, "Please, join us and order what you like."

Darcash settled Alamina in her seat and took a chair next to her.

Darcash looked at her with solemn eyes. "Are you the only one in your line?"

"I am one of a line of daughters born to dragons. My grandmother, Charani, is your daughter. My mother, Lolli, gets a lot of her colouring from you. She has your hair."

He sat back as he heard that his family line went beyond him and his wife. "A line of daughters."

Alamina cocked her head. "Have you met my father?"

Zora made a face. "Yes. That is how I ended up here. He traded his blood—meaning me—for an insult to King Olvadi. No one ever did give me the details."

"I hate what Alfonso made me into, but I could not imagine life without Darcash."

Darcash smiled. "She paced the shoreline every night for three months before I walked out of the surf to speak with her. When we coupled and the energy flared between us, I was sure she was my mate. She disappeared for a few months and I didn't think anything of it, but when she disappeared again for two decades, I became concerned. I followed her and found her battling a nest of vampires in defense of a young woman. I destroyed the vampires and the young woman escaped, but Alamina was mortally wounded. I took her home and nursed her back to health. We have been together ever since."

Alamina smiled as she admitted, "I checked up on my girls via a scrying mirror. I always suspected you were doing well, though I was concerned about your mother. She was a wild one."

Regick chuckled. "The entire family will be here this week. I have set aside an upper floor of suites for you, and you can have the run of the building and the city if you wish."

Alamina brightened. "They will?"

"I called them all and asked them if they would come to bless the mating between Zora and myself."

Zora smiled. "He really did. He didn't

know if any of you would show."

Alamina smiled a beatific smile. "I was born a dhampir, which should have made me sterile. A dragon gave me a chance to have a child, and that daughter gave me the strength to train her into being a survivor. She did the same for her daughter, and she did the same for you. It has been quite a legacy."

Zora sat back and ordered her dessert, smiling beatifically at part of her history sitting in front of her and bickering with each other on who wanted to have dinner and which one wanted a snack.

Regick could order what he wanted, she would have what she wanted and they would both end up in the same bed at night. It was strange when she began thinking about the future and could see compromises now made for possibilities later.

Regick slid toward her until his thigh

touched hers under the table. He grinned. "Our first family meal."

"You aren't counting Charani at the diner."

He turned toward her and she kissed him softly. "I won't run. Baby or not. I won't run, Regick."

He blinked and wove his hand through her hair, kissing frantically at her lips, cheeks and eyes. When he finished, he pressed his forehead to hers and he whispered, "Thank you."

"I am much more the type to make your life a living hell, love." She smiled.

He put his arm around her. They chatted with her relatives until dessert arrived.

Zora was halfway through it when she had a thought and looked at Regick. "How do I buy a vampire?"

The table erupted in uproar, and Zora sat there listening to the riot explode around her. For the first time in her life, she was at a proper family dinner and she had picked a fight. Grinning, she turned her attention to the crème brulee and listened to the arguments for and against purchasing a vampire.

It was nice to be part of a family and have a future... even if it was looking to be completely bizarre.

Author's Note

This story is the prequel to *One Part Human*. The characters will pop up during the *An Obscure Magic* series, and I hope that I will keep consistency. My fingers are crossed. ☺

Thanks for reading,

Viola Grace

About the Author

Viola Grace (aka Zenina Masters) is a Canadian sci-fi/paranormal romance writer with ambitions to keep writing for the rest of her life. She specializes in short stories because the thrill of discovery, of all those firsts, is what keeps her writing.

An artist who enjoys a story that catches you up, whirls you around and sets you down with a smile on your face is all she endeavours to be. She prefers to leave the drama to those who are better suited to it, she always goes for the cheap laugh.